W9-DBZ-228

This book belongs to

_____

This book is dedicated to my children – Mikey, Kobe, and Jojo. We all feel anger sometimes and that's normal. What makes the difference is how we manage it.

Angry Ninja

By Mary Nhin   Pictures By Jelena Stupar

"Give it back!" screamed Angry Ninja.

His little sister had used his jumprope without asking and it made Angry Ninja furious.

Angry Ninja could feel his throat tighten, his heart beat faster, and his breathing start to get heavy.

He felt as if he was going to scream any second.

It wasn't fun being upset and having everyone mad at you. But Angry Ninja just didn't know how to control his emotions.

Later that day, Positive Ninja came over to hang out with Angry Ninja.

PLAYER 1   PLAYER 2
    4   -   18

They decided to play a game of PIG. Until
Angry Ninja got upset when he was losing.

And guess what happened?

The two talked about it.

Positive Ninja explained, "Anger is normal. It's how you deal with it that makes a difference. There's something I do and it's super easy."

"I use the 1 + 3 + 10. I say 1 calm word like 'Relax'. You could say, 'Breathe'. Then, I take 3 slow, deep breaths. Finally, I count to 10," said Positive Ninja.

After I've calmed down, I add an 'I am _____' statement.
Like if my sister broke my toy, I might say,

Afterwards, Angry Ninja went inside to get some chocolate cake his mom had made.

When he found out his sister ate the very last slice...

Angry Ninja started to clench his fists, but then he remembered what Positive Ninja said.

And do you know what happened next?

Angry Ninja said to himself, "Breathe."
He took 3 slow, deep breaths.

Breathe...

1, 2, 3...
...

Then, counted to 10.

It worked!
He felt...strangely good.

A simple strategy to stay calm could become your secret weapon for managing anger.

Sign up for new Ninja book releases at GrowGrit.co

📷 @marynhin @GrowGrit
#NinjaLifeHacks

f Mary Nhin   Grow Grit

▶ Grow Grit

Made in the USA
Middletown, DE
15 June 2020